I0738523

A Thin Line Between Love & Obsession
~Special Edition~

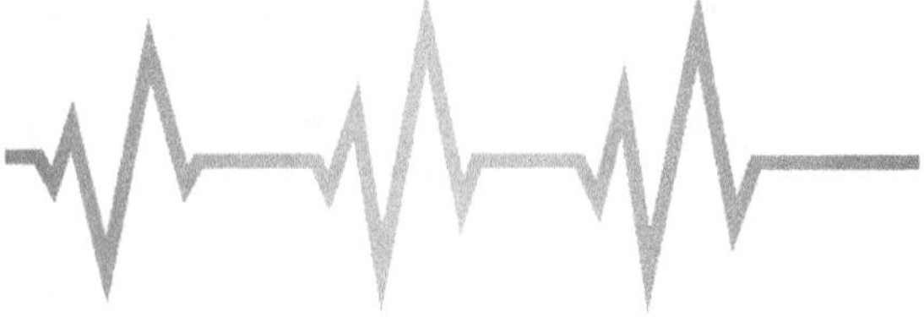

Erica T. Capri

A Thin Line Between Love &Obsession
~Special Edition~

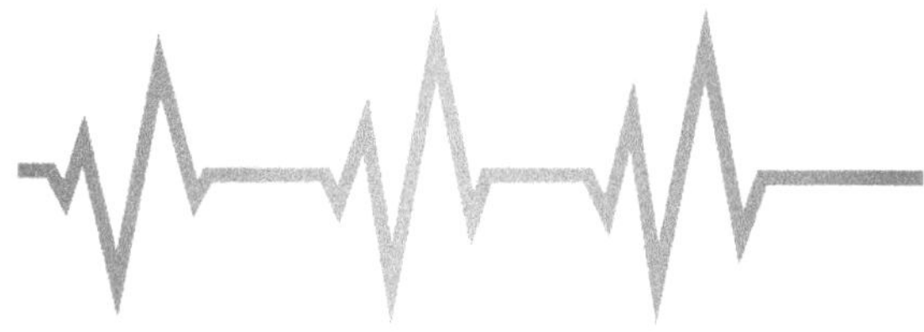

Erica T. Capri

Gemlight Publishing LLC
Gulfport, Mississippi

This book is dedicated to my heavenly father and everyone who supported my writing endeavors.

In Loving Memory of...

Sherman Walls (Grandfather)
Mary Walls (Grandmother)
Annie Faye Sherrill (Grandmother)

A Thin Line Between Love & Obsession
~Special Edition~

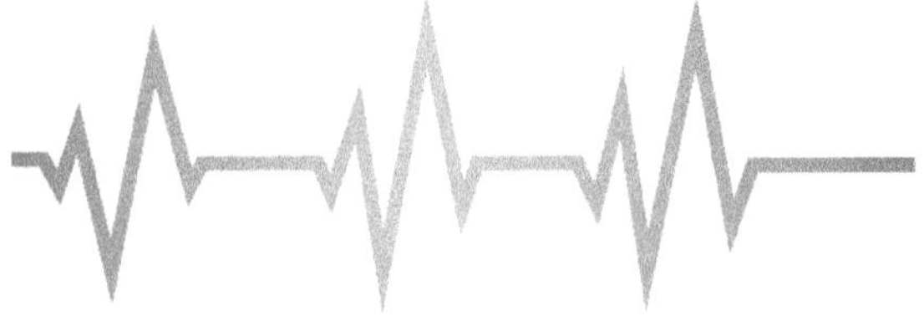

Erica T. Capri

Prologue

Love and Obsession is a thin line. When we are in love, we think about the person all the time. This is the infatuation stage. The infatuation stage of romantic love usually occurs in the early months in a relationship. The love relationship usually evolves over time such that it no longer involves the near desperate intensity and fervor of infatuation. At some point in our lives, we struggle to differentiate between love and obsession, especially if you don't love yourself or have self-worth, you cannot love others. You will not be able to love others, if you have no compassion for yourself. Love is composed of a single soul inhabiting two bodies. Love is

what we are born with. Fear of love is what we have experience. The spiritual journey vis the unlearning of fear an acceptance of love back into our hearts. It can also be dangerous and cloud our mind with judgment that can easily turn into obsession; the line is just that close. I would know, because I experienced it.

My name is Kendall Alexandra. I am a thirty-five-year-old Christian woman, and at one point, I thought I had it all. For two years, I was married to the top district attorney in the city of New Orleans, Larry Alexander. The first year of our marriage, we gave birth to a little girl. Sadly, she died the same day she was born. After her death, Larry and I kept trying to conceive another child, but it kept leading to multiple disappointments. Being a woman who suffered through so much—not being able to bear my husband a child—I became depressed. After the incident, I began to attend church and get my life right with God, but Larry didn't. He began to distant himself from me, which led to many lonely nights – celebrating holidays, and special occasions alone. Larry and I are very wealthy, but the pride that Larry carries, and his controlling spirit caused me to question my marriage. Battling with self-worth, I knew a change was going to have to come.

I grew up without a mother and father. Raising myself, I knew this wasn't the life I wanted, but Larry swept me off my feet, took me off the streets and now I'm living a life of bondage and being controlled. I had never been close to any other man, other than my husband, so I knew that self-worth was my weakness and random encounters with others has the ability to confuse me. I'm a living witness of trails and triumph. I found myself battling between love & obsession.

This is my story...

Chapter ONE

"Oh, my god!" I exclaimed once I took a good look at my reflection in the mirror.

"What?" Larry asked from beside me, confused, while tying his tie.

"Do it look like I pick up a few pounds? Do I look Fat?" I said as I looked over my body once again.

Larry sighed, clearly out of frustration. "Unless you're talking about the thickness in your ass, I don't believe you are" He pauses for a moment before walking over to stand behind me, staring at my reflection in the mirror.

He wraps his arms around me from behind. "Besides, I hardly think any woman with nice curves, a small waist like yours would think they are fat."

He gives me a squeeze, kisses me on the cheek and slaps me on my butt, with a smirk.

When he releases me, I turn and glare at him.

"Hush! I can't believe nothing you tell me, since I know you are the 'King-of-lies' whom feeding me more lies."

He flashes me a smile and quickly leaves the room, shaking his head. I laugh it off like always. I'm used to him walking away from me with a nonchalant attitude.

I turned back around to face the big mirror in my bedroom, studying my appearance. My brown hair flowed down around my face in deep waves. My face looked fresh and natural with the slightest hint of makeup I'd put on. I was wearing a red fitted dress that hugged my curves perfectly. It was sexy, yet classy, but I wasn't used to showing off my body. I always felt uncomfortable wearing clothes like this that showed more skin than I was used to. Sometimes I feel insecure about my body, even though there is no reason for me to feel that way. But today I wanted to see a change for a split moment. I wanted Larry to see me in a sexy dress, hoping he would've wanted to take me out to lunch like we use to. But my wish wasn't granted as usual, so I took the dress off and slipped on my work-out clothes.

"Linda, I'm going to the gym. Be back in one hour," I said loudly, so that Linda would hear me from the laundry room as I head to my front door.

"Okay, dear. Don't forget your dry cleaning pick up in thirty minutes."

I roll my eyes at her reply. What a pest! I thought.

"Oh, don't forget to buy some Uncle Ben's rice for me, Kendall ...Oh, and I'd also appreciate it if you bought me some corn candy, too." Linda spoke loudly from the other room.

I snickered. "Whatever!" I yelled sarcastically over my shoulder.

Linda shouted back. "For once it seemed like we might be on same page. I was hoping you would bring back what I asked for this time."

Linda, my housekeeper, never lets me forget anything. Sometimes I feel like she is the mother I never had. Larry hired Linda as a full-time live-in two years ago to keep an eye on me. I had lost a child that I was told I couldn't carry. As a result of the tragedy, I was diagnosed with Dysthymia, a chronic depressive disorder. I've gotten tired of the same ole simple life, so I want to try having another child, but Larry refuses to try anymore after I had multiple miscarriages. It has been six months now, and I've decided to try something new. I joined the gym where Carol has been going to for years. Being at the gym gives me a sense of relief, a sense of peace. It allows me the time and opportunity to think, while I work out my frustrations at the same time.

I chuckle before closing the door behind me, heading to my car. After a short ten-minute drive, I arrive at the gym, and soon enough, I am in workout mode. After about thirty-five minutes of working out and chatting with Carol, we had finished our workout. I gathered my things and headed toward the door, while reaching in my bag to answer my annoying, ringing cell phone. Suddenly, with no warning, all my items that I held in my hand went flying to the ground.

In my hasty distraction to retrieve my items, I encountered the double doors of the gym, or so I thought.

"Darn it! Watch where you're going!" I heard a cocky, yet sexy, voice say.

"Excuse me? If I'm not mistaken, you bumped into me! Not the other way around, mister." I stooped to gather my things, still reaching for my ringing phone, which was now also on the ground, but it stopped before I could answer it. After carefully examining it for any damage, I silently, thank God that it is still intact.

He stoops next to me and kindly helps me pick my things up off the ground. I briefly take a glance at the cocky stranger for the first time. Oh, dear God...My heart starts beating double-time. This man was just too handsome, too sexy, and too HOT for his own good.

He glanced at me.

"You must not be from around here, because a pretty lady like you shouldn't be alone in this neighborhood. Not with an attitude like yours. You could have bumped into a robber or something, even though I steal hearts." He smiled at me like I had never been smiled at before.

I was really trying hard to focus on what he was saying, but I was just too busy checking him out. From his seductive eyes, to his full lips that left me surprisingly breathless. My eyes went down to his chest and torso. He was wearing a gray muscle shirt. My mouth started watering as I glimpsed his six-pack through the too little shirt. That man was so fine.

"Well, I guess now you want to ignore a brother," he said, giving me a long stare.

That snapped me out of my thoughts and I silently asked God to forgive me for lusting over this man and his sexiness.

"Robber in a gym, really? I guess it was my fault," I admitted. "Please forgive me and excuse me, I must go home to my husband," I replied nervously, trying hard to keep my eyes off the attractive man in front of me.

He looked at me confused, as if he wanted to say something. Then he shook his head and began to walk away. "You have a great day with your husband," he said over his shoulder, sarcastically.

He must have noticed me looking at him in an inappropriate way. Especially, since he now knows I am married, since I mentioned my husband.

Feeling embarrassed, I turned in the opposite direction without saying a single word. Well, that was so weird! I thought. Sighing, I quickly head to my car without any other incident. Thank God!

While driving home after finishing all my errands, I couldn't help but replay the incident from earlier inside my head. I scrunched up my face at the thought. I couldn't believe how I was lusting over another man. After the numerous Bible classes my pastor taught us about lusting, I never knew what it really meant until today. I instantly began praying in my spirit and shook my head to clear my train of thoughts. It doesn't matter anyways. I'm sure I'll never see him again.

Chapter **TWO**

"I'm back!" I yelled, walking into the house. "What's for dinner? I asked Linda as I walked into the kitchen and dropped my keys and cell phone on the granite countertop.

"Pot roast with steamed broccoli," Linda said, peering inside the oven.

"Awesome! Thank you so much. You're an angel, Linda." I gave her a sweet smile.

Three seconds later, I heard Carol walking through my door. Carol and I had been best friends for ten years now. Ever since the first time we met in college we have never been apart, even though we are complete opposites of each other. Where she is tall and skinny as a model, I, on the other hand, have a very curvy frame. Carol is very outspoken and loves to party. The only thing Carol and I have in common is we both are licensed accountants; which Carol pursued and for me I'm just a housewife. Which I get reminded of every time Carol comes over to visit me.

"I'm home for dinner, honey." Carol giggled all the way to the table. If ever there was a moment for me to slap Carol, it would have been then. I knew what she was doing. Carol has this thing about Larry. She hates him, and says that I live like a desperate housewife, waiting for him to come home for dinner.

"Shut up, Carol, not today." I was not in the mood for her foolishness today.

Even though Carol is annoying at times, she is my best friend, so I do listen to what she has to say. Although I didn't want to admit it, a lot of what she said was true. I could count the number of times that Larry and I had dinner together. He is an attorney, which requires him to work many long hours. I Guess? Plus, he travels a lot.

Carol brings me back to reality with another smart comment.

"I just wanted to say that, since you never hear it from your wonderful husband," Carol replied with a grin.

After dinner, Carol and I discussed me getting a job. She told me that her job now has a new owner and they are looking for another experienced accountant. "You really should come by tomorrow for an interview," she said. I was skeptical about it at first, but as I think back on how much I love accounting, I accepted her offer. "Great! Nine o'clock sharp, and please wear some heels, honey," Carol said as she walks out my front door.

After a long sleepless night of tossing and turning, morning had come. I awoke to the annoying smell of a woman's cheap perfume and liquor, mixed with peppermint mouthwash from Larry's shirt that he obviously took off an hour ago when he came in. I groaned as I stretched to get out of bed, then kneeled to say my morning prayer. Today was my first day back in the workforce, or so I hoped. I have always loved working in accounting, but when we got married, Larry didn't want me to work at all. Out of the two years we've been married, I've spent my days going to yoga classes, shopping, reading, going to church and watching movies ALONE.

With a determined, but lazy yawn, I stood up and went to my bathroom.

After a relaxing shower, I walked out of the bathroom with a towel hugging my body and went to look for the perfect outfit to wear to the interview. Larry jumps out of bed and comes over to me with a look in his eyes I had never seen before. "Where are you going, dear? he asked, pouring on the charm. Maybe to make me forget that he had only gotten home a few hours earlier.

"I have an interview today, at the office where Carol works."

He looks at me and responds by telling me that I'm not going, and no wife of his is going to work for another man.

I was puzzled.

"Kendra get back in bed, you're not going to work for nobody, now or never, no exceptions," Larry said. I looked at him and continued getting dress. After settling down with dark blue slacks, a nice Michael Kors cream colored top, along with cute beige heels, and Michael Kors purse, I was finally dressed. When I was done, I started doing my hair and put on a little bit of mascara and lip gloss. Looking in the mirror, I felt satisfied with my appearance. I was thankful and ready to begin another blessed day.

Walking out the bathroom was all I remembered. At that moment, it felt like I had walked into a brick wall. Larry had slapped me so hard I almost became unconscious. He ripped my clothes off, threw me back on the bed and told me not to go anywhere. I was terrified to know that he's bold enough to start back with the physical abuse toward me. He took me by surprise, and his actions caused many evil thoughts to rush through my head.

"I can't believe this! Are you crazy? Insane? Or are you just doing this to frustrate me and prevent me from having a normal life?" I asked him as he glared back at me. I was so angry I was shaking. But I refused to back down.

"I am not going to allow you to dictate my career, and I certainly will not let you put your hands on me again! Any man who would do that is the kind with no fear of God, and no dignity. Just like YOU!" Those words clearly were a surprise to him and pushed him over the edge. Shock registered across his face. He was so angry.

"You're just so..." Just as he began to counteract back at me, Linda walks into the room.

"You guys should stop fighting. There's nothing worth arguing about on such a beautiful blessed day."

Larry snapped his head toward Linda. "What I do in my house is none of your business!"

Linda huffed and muttered a "Whatever" before walking away, leaving Larry and I staring at her.

I changed into another shirt and headed out the door before telling Larry not to bother coming home tonight. He looked at me with guilt written all over his face, attempting to stop me and apologize. But I didn't want to hear anything he had to say.

I got into my car and drove off, thinking back on my near-death experience one year ago, when Larry and I had a terrible fight. I was almost killed and had a miscarriage in the midst of it. That wasn't the first time Larry felt like making me his punching bag when things don't go his way. It became so normal I would go to bed with several layers of clothing to protect myself from his abuse. Tears began rolling down my face as I thought back to all the promises, he made that he would never put his hands on me ever again after the loss of our child.

When I arrived at the business, I looked in the rear-view mirror and noticed that my makeup was smeared. So, I freshened it up before I walked into the building. Carol met me at the door, rushing me to come in. She explained that she had covered for me until I got there.

"I hope you have a very good reason for being late; the owner's son has been waiting for you," Carol said, looking me up and down for approval, then smoothing down a strand of my hair.

"You don't want to know what happened," I said with a look of worry on my face. I sat there contemplating on what I would say when the owner asked why I am late? or why should he hire me? etc. Feeling ashamed, I held my head down, saying a silent prayer. Then I got out my resume and ran a hand across my hair to make sure it was still intact. Suddenly, I stopped what I was doing when I heard a manly familiar voice.

"Hello, I'm Mr. Kodak. I'm the Administrator Director."

I looked towards the source of the voice and then my eyes landed on him – the handsome, attractive, annoying man from the gym yesterday.

"Lord have mercy .... Jesus have mercy!"

Chapter THREE

Crap, what now? Maybe he doesn't remember me. Just keep calm, keep calm!

"Mr. Scott Kodak, and your name is?" he asked as he reached out to shake my hand, gazing into my eyes. I was totally in shock, but finally, I snapped out of my thoughts.

"Kendall Alexandra. It's a pleasure to meet you, Mr. Kodak," I said, wondering if he really didn't remember me.

He nodded, inviting me to take a seat in a comfortable looking chair across from his desk. I sat down and shuffled the papers in my lap, glancing around at his tastefully decorated office. Once he was seated in his oversized leather chair, I reached across his desk and handed him my resume. He takes it and places it neatly on his desk. Then he leaned back in his chair and clasped his hands together without even glancing at my resume. His eyes were focused intensely on me.

"Okay, Mrs. Alexandra, this is not like an ordinary interview. I'll get straight to the point. I will ask you a few questions, and if all your answers are yes, I will hire you. First, do you know how to conduct an audit? Can you do income tax returns on all types of businesses? Can you advise a new business how to set up an accounting system? And lastly, can you work some twelve hours shifts, if needed during peak season?"

"Yes, of course. I can do them all," I replied.

His features slowly relaxed, and he watched me intensely with his brown eyes, gazing deep into my eyes as if he was making sure I was being genuine.

"Good," a small smirk came over his face as he continued, "because I need a real woman that means business." As he talked, he walked over and sat on the edge of his desk right in front of me. He was so close I could smell the provocative scent of his cologne. "Boy you are so fine, I don't mind you kissing me!"

I sighed and gave him a small, unsure smile. "Well, does that mean you're my new boss? Because I'm just that type of woman."

After a few seconds, his big warm hand rubbed my shoulder. "You're hired! Welcome to the team." He flashed his pearly white smile again.

"Oh, Jesus take the wheel"

I let out a sigh of relief. "Thank you. You won't regret it. I'll do my best to make you proud." I beamed in excitement.

"Okay, we're done here. How about we go get a bite somewhere? I'm hungry," Scott exclaimed, handing me my resume as we walked towards the door.

"Sorry, I can't. My husband won't approve of that," I said as we exited his office.

Scott stopped in his tracks. "Hold up, that sounds familiar." He runs his hand across his chin, deep in thought. We automatically look at each other at the same time. I scowled at him, while he just smirked.

"You're the lady from the gym?"

"Gym? Not possible, not me!"

I rolled my eyes and then looked away. He laughs. "Great, this is going to be fun. See you next week, Mrs. Alexandra!" Scott said as he chuckled. Then he winked before walking away from me.

For a few seconds, I didn't know what to say. Then a slight smile came over my face. Oh, so he thinks he has power over me now? I thought. Well, technically he did, since he was my new boss, but still, I'm waiting on him with the sword of the Lord–my Bible. He might not know it, but as long as I continue to pray and stay in touch with God, he can't touch this.

Feeling relieved – because I got the job – and angry at the same time – because of all that had happened this morning – I decided to go shopping for a new wardrobe. I sighed just as I finally got outside, taking a deep breath of fresh air. I started to feel free and all my troubles had disappeared.

As hungry as I was, I had to remind my-self that I am married and it would not be a good look, to be seen eating out with your boss when you're just getting started in the work-force again. If I had not been running late, and if Larry hadn't been acting a fool this morning, I probably would have had time to eat break-fast, I thought. By the time I made it to the job, it was a relief just to still be alive. On my way to the office, I came within inches of ramming into the back of a red truck, had run two red lights, and a whole lot of stop signs, and still didn't make it on time. So, just the thought that I got the job was enough to make me want to shout and praise God.

After five hours of shopping, I had a major headache from not eating. But pulling into my driveway relieved a lot of pressure. As I walked into my house, there was Linda, standing at the top of my stairs, looking at me with her hands on her hips. She looked so much like my granny it almost made me laugh.

"Linda, please don't start."

"Why more clothes, Kendall? It won't solve your problems. Spending money shopping all the time is not the answer. Why can't you con-trol yourself?" Linda reprimanded.

I tightened my jaws. First, all the drama I went through this morning, now Linda nagging about me shopping. I wasn't going to have it today.

"Linda, not today., please go to you side of the house after you get me a glass of wine," I said walking up the stairs, wobbling from the exhaustion I got from shopping.

Chapter FOUR

After an hour of settling in from my long day, I began my evening devotional reading. I heard a chirping noise coming from my phone, letting me know I have a message coming through.

The text message was from an unfamiliar number.

Hi, beautiful, I hope you enjoying your day because we have a long day next week.

Scott K2blessed (smiles)

It was a text from Scott, as I looked at the

text unimaginable thoughts surged through my mind. I didn't know if I should respond to the text or continue reading my devotion. After thinking for ten minutes, I responded back saying.

Okay, thanks, can't wait.

As soon as I sent the message, Scott responded immediately, as though he was waiting for my response. It said:

What are you doing for the weekend?

Reading the text, a voice resonated in my head, telling me to cut it off right now before it went any further. So, I obeyed the voice and began to pray. I went to sleep, hoping for a better tomorrow.

Drifting into a deep sleep, flashes of Scott invade my thoughts while I slept. I jumped up out of my bed and went downstairs to get a glass of water. Just as I emptied my glass, Larry came walking through the door at two o'clock in the morning as usual, smelling like cheap perfume with liquor on his breath, mixed with peppermint. I could tell he was surprised to see me up.

"Hey, baby, why you up so late?" Larry avoided my eyes, trying to avoid making eye contact.

"I couldn't sleep," I said. I went to my bedroom to go back to sleep. Larry followed behind me, apologizing for yesterday, giving me these 'I'm sorry' quotes until he went sound asleep. Praying in my spirit, I was hoping that he wouldn't give me trouble next week when I got up for work. Finally, I fell into a deep sleep that put me at ease.

Saturday came and I spent it at home doing nothing but watching re-runs of The Haves and the Have Nots and eating whatever I was craving. During the whole day, I couldn't stop thinking about if I should've responded back to Scott's text message. Larry had left to go out to the track with the boys for a 'pimp your ride' contest. Sometimes I can't help but wonder if I'm married to a single man that say he's my husband. Everything Larry buys is for single men. Even the men he hangs out with are single. It is our anniversary and he is out with the boys, while I'm at home watching #HAHN#.

My thoughts about my husband were cut

short by the sound of my phone chirping, indicating I had a text message. I grabbed my phone from my coffee table.

It was a text from Scott again that said:

Hey, Kendall! What are you up to?

I smiled as I texted him back, wondering why he keeps trying to communicate with me.

Hey! Just sitting around doing housework.

A few seconds later, my phone beeped again.

Wow, do you want me to come rescues you from the lion's den, and have some dinner? :) I won't take no for an answer.

After reading the text, I was tempted to accept the invite, but I knew it was totally against my standards. I would be doing just like in the Bible. Ephesians 4:27 tells us not to give the devil room to enter into your life. Not saying Scott is the devil, but I have to guard myself. Even though he might be doing it for the right reason, other people may not see that. So, I responded back.

I wasn't planning on going anywhere.

I slid down on my couch, shaking my head, contemplating on whether I should go or not. Then he responded back with:

Is it because you never went out with a male friend? Look, I just want to take you out to get to know you, no strings attached, even your husband can join us.

I text him back.

I'll pass on the invite, I have to get ready for church tomorrow. You have a goodnight, Scott.

His reply took only seconds to arrive.

Okay, beautiful! Goodnight!

I drifted off the sleep on my sofa, thanking God for giving me the strength to overcome temptation.

<><><>

I didn't hear anything from Scott for the rest of the weekend. Maybe he's starting to respect my boundaries, I thought. Before I knew it, my weekend was over, I had an awesome time at church and I was ready for work on Monday, ready to start a new week.

Direct my path, oh God.

I did my morning routine, which including prayer, working out at the gym, taking a hot shower, putting on clothes, and going downstairs to eat breakfast. I grabbed my bag and my car keys, ready to head to work. The drive from my house to the office was about thirty minutes, so I turned on the radio to entertain me on the road.

"All of your problems, all of your pains, lay it down, lay it down. All of your heartache, all guilt and shame, lay it down, lay it down. Cast your cares upon him, he'll hear your call, lay it down, lay it down."

I sang along with Troy Sneed the entire drive to work. I enjoyed passing through all the lights, passing the parks, watching loving couples, and kids walking to school. Listening to that song just put me in a joyous moment. I arrived at the parking lot outside my new job. I can't remember the last time I was excited to go to work until today. I pulled into a parking space and put my car in park. Before I could shut off my engine, there stood Carol, waiting on me outside the passenger door, smiling.

"Hey, chick, are you ready to make things happen this morning?" Carol asked, grinning.

"Yes, ma'am, I'm very excited about this job," I exclaimed, showing my pearly whites in a big smile. "Well, good, because Mr. Kodak wants us to bring in at least ten new clients today," Carol said as she helped me grab my bag out of my back seat.

"Whoa!" I gave her a surprised look.

As we walked into the main office, Carol directed me to my office. Walking down the classical fresh-smelling hallway, I saw Scott Kodak seated at his desk, talking on the phone, wearing a nice stitched designer two-piece charcoal suit with a blue colored shirt, which seemed to make him look even more attractive than the first time I saw him. Scott looked in my eyes and raised his hand, signaling for us to come into his office. Carol opened his door as I let myself in, looking at Scott. He had a big smile on his face as he ended his phone conversation, which, by the sound of it, seemed to be his father.

Scott Kodak stood up from his chair and walked around his desk, before leaning against it, facing us.

"Good morning, ladies. Please have a seat before we get started with our morning meeting," he ordered, which we quickly followed. "So, let me start by telling you how much I appreciate you both for being on time this morning," Scott said, sarcastically, looking over at me. I looked at him in a shameful way as he begins lecturing us during the meeting. Fifteen minutes into the meeting, Scott began discussing the new accounts coming in and that Kodak Enterprise would need as many new clients as possible. The answer No would not be an option for him. Instantly, I had a flashback to the words of my old professor: Live life with a purpose, not a pain. I guess hearing Scott speaking made me realize I have not been living a purpose-filled life. As the meeting ended, I grabbed my purse and my notepad where I had carefully written down the notes from the meeting, then Carol and I began walking toward the door.

"Excuse me, Mrs. Alexandra. Can I see you for a split second?" Scott's voice was blank, his face expressionless. My heartbeat quickened at the sound of his voice. I looked at Carol; she had this weird, startled expression on her face, which made me nervous. I slowly turned around, acknowledging his request, trying to keep my focus on anything but him.

"I hope you will allow me to take you to lunch, since I couldn't rescue you over the weekend." Scott's deep voice triggered something inside me, making it impossible for me to ignore him. I was so startled, I couldn't say anything. There was an awkward silence as he waited for me to respond.

"Okay, that didn't get anywhere," Scott

replied. "Can you make an appointment for me Thursday at 10:30 a.m.?" he asked in a clear voice. "It's a house call for one of our biggest clients."

"Umm... Yeah, sure, I can do both," I replied, searching for the notepad to write down the appointment. My hands trembled from nervousness, causing all of my papers, my purse and everything in it to spill onto the floor. I quickly knelt down to grab all the items before Scott could see my prescription pill bottle of antidepressant medication.

Scott kindly reached down to help me pick up my items. I was so embarrassed as we stared into each other's eyes. Snapping out of the moment, we heard Carol's voice coming through Scott's intercom, telling him he has a call on line one. Scott and I quickly stood up and put some distance between us, while I slipped my pill bottle back in my purse, hoping he didn't see it. At that moment, I realized I had been in the most awkward situations over the past few days.

"Oh, let me get this," Scott said, before rubbing my shoulder softly. "I'll see you at lunch," he whispered, staring deeply into my eyes, then he turned and left without saying another word. I mumbled okay and started walking toward the door, holding my purse and notepad close to my stomach, squeezing my eyes shut, trying to clear my head for work. Just as I managed to open my eyes, I was grabbed with FORCE and pushed into the wall of the hallway.

God! I shall fear no EVIL!

C hapter SIX

"Kendall! Kendall! Are you okay?" I could hear the concern in Carol's voice as she assisted me in getting up off the floor. As she reached to help me up, I was confused, trying to figure out what just happened. It's like I was hearing Larry's voice from a distance. Still dazed and confused, Carol tells me that Larry came into the office drunk and pissed off. Obviously, after witnessing the exchange between Scott and me, he slammed me against the wall and began to choke me until I became unconscious.

"The police took him away in handcuffs and we issued a restraining order, barring him from coming near the job," Carol replied. I wiped the tears from my eyes as she explained everything to me. My hands trembled with fear. Larry was in a rage and had attacked me again. But once again, I had narrowly escaped.

Still trembling, I stumbled to the entrance of my office as Carol assisted me. "What a jerk!" Carol said.

"Why is he doing this to me?" I asked Carol. Of course, Carol went on a rant about me getting a divorce from Larry. How he is hurting me more than he is helping me and telling me that law enforcement granted me to stay away from my house for twenty-four hours. As Carol is telling me all these things, I can feel the rush of a panic attack coming over my body. My heart was rapidly pounding in my chest, pumping so fast I felt the rush of my blood flowing through my veins. My vision became blurry and I began to black out. I felt like breaking down to my knees, crying, believing that my job has ended from the chaos I caused today.

Carol reached into my purse quickly to give me my medication before Scott came back in the building. He had exited the building to give the report to the police. When Scott reentered the building, he came into my office to make sure I was okay. He held his finger to my lips to silence my explanation of what happened.

"No need to explain, just take the rest of the day off," he said, lightly pulling me into his arms to give me a reassuring hug. His hands patted up and down my body, heatedly.

"Thank you." I gave a weak smile of relief as he smiled back at me. Then I remembered Carol telling me I couldn't go back home. I felt a sense of vulnerability not knowing where I was going to sleep. I couldn't go to Carol's apartment because that's the first place Larry would look for me. I knew he would also check every hotel in the area searching for me. Feeling a sense of worry, while all these thoughts ran through my mind, I was interrupted by Scott's voice.

"You can stay at our company cottage, which is twenty-five miles outside of the city."

As bad as I wanted to turn down the offer, I had no choice but to take it. But before I could reply, Carol answered for me. "Yes, she sure will stay there tonight." I smiled at Scott, reassuring that I agreed with her answer.

Just as Scott left to get everything prepared for my stay at the cottage, my phone rang. When I picked up my phone, Larry's photo and name was displayed on the screen, notifying me he was calling, so I pressed the reject button over thirty times in a row. Larry had become a little obsessed over me within these past few days. It felt like some demons have taken control of him and he was afraid of losing me. While continually pressing reject, I start thinking about a time when my Bishop at the church preached about a marriage being 'Unequally Yoked'. He explained that no marriage would last if one was going in one direction and the other person was pulling in another. Marriage is a team, and it takes a team to win.

After thinking about that, I started to see the big picture. We were never a team. Finally, after thirty-five attempts to reach me, Larry stopped calling. So, I put my phone down to go to the restroom to clear my head once again.

Scott stopped me in the hallway to give me the information. He handed me the paper with the address, security code and a credit card so that I could get a few items I would need during my stay. With a thankful heart, I embraced him, relieved that he had thought of everything. As I hugged him, the scent of his cologne was intoxicating, leaving me breathless. Softly, he placed his hand under my chin and lifted my face to his, moving slowly toward my lips. I was stunned, knowing what he was about to do. Gently, he leaned in and placed a soft warm kiss on my cheek, making me feel like a million dollars.

"You are so beautiful," he whispered, gazing into my eyes. "Call me if you need me." Scott gave me a seductive smile before turning and going back into his office.

"Okay," I replied as I rushed to the bathroom, smiling.

Traveling thirty minutes out to the cottage, I finally made it. This cottage was on the countryside out in the middle of nowhere. After punching in the security code at the gate, I pulled into the driveway. It was indescribable; it was more than a cottage, it looked like a mini-villa. The landscaping was beautiful. Magnificent palm trees stood on each side of the cottage's entrance and the lawn was nicely kept with beautiful flowers everywhere. I just felt a sense of peace. I put my car in park, took the keys out of the ignition and stepped outside my car door. I walked toward the front entrance of the house, still in awe of its beauty. As I put the key in the door to unlock it, I entered a four-bedroom cleaned white-walled home. On the far left was a 52" flat screen TV mounted on the wall with beautiful pictures surrounding each area, and on the table was a bottle of expensive Verity Le Desir, Sonoma wine and a glass sitting on top of the table with a note that read: ENJOY THE MOMENT!

With a smirk on my face, and feeling relieved for the moment, I walked into one of the bedrooms. In there was a huge king-sized bed, similar to the one I have in my bedroom. I knew then I was going to get a goodnight's rest, so I flopped on the bed as I threw off my shoes. Once I was comfortable, I reached for the remote and turned on the TV, surfing through every network and channel, looking for something to watch that interests me. I finally dozed off to sleep with the remote in my hand.

Three hours had gone by when the sound of my phone woke me up, notifying me I had fifteen missed calls and six text messages. Assuming it was Larry, I reached over and grabbed my phone off the nightstand to turn it off. Rubbing my eyes, trying to stay awake, I went into the bathroom. Standing in front of the mirror, I could see every pain I'd experienced on my face, so I grabbed a towel to wash my face and started running water to take a shower.

After ten minutes relaxing, letting the water flow all over my body, I finally stepped out the shower and wrapped a plush bath towel around my body. Then I walked towards the kitchen to pour me some wine. Just as I entered, Scott was walking through the door.

"Lord have mercy!" I screamed and jumped back so he wouldn't see any parts of my body. "Holy Crap!" In my haste to retreat, I bumped the wine glass against the counter and watched as it tumbled towards the floor. Fortunately, it didn't break. Scott caught it before it hit the floor. "Good reflex," I said to Scott for rescuing me from making another mess.

"You know, I think I make you pretty nervous." Scott looked at me intensely. "You didn't respond to any of my texts or calls. I was worried, that's why I came by."

"You can't just pop up like this, Scott." I felt embarrassed once again.

"I wouldn't be here if you had responded back. You are on my property and it's my responsibility to keep you safe." Scott's tone was aggressive. He just stood there, looking at me for a full thirty seconds, saying nothing.

"Scott, what's wrong? Is everything all right?" He was making me nervous. The look in his eyes was making me blush. I pulled the towel tighter around my body.

"I see why your husband is obsessed with you and going crazy."

"He doesn't trust me."

"Oh, really? Have you given him any reason?"

"No, his insecurity stems from his cheating." I shrugged. "I guess he feels if he's doing it, I'm doing it. This is the closest I've ever been to another man in over five years."

"Well, as beautiful as you are, I just can't imagine." Scott flashed me another smile and held up his hands. "As you see, I brought dinner as well," he said, lowering his eyes toward my body.

"Whoa! I see that. Let me go put on some clothes."

"Please, ma'am, this is too epic!" He chuckled.

As I walked back in the bedroom, I felt Scott's eyes on me the entire time, so I moved with haste. Moment like this is when I need my Bible by my side. So, I quickly kneeled and prayed for strength to endure the temptation that has been sent my way. After praying a good five minutes, I was interrupted by Scott screaming out, asking me if I'm okay. So, I closed my prayer and slipped on a pair of red silk pajamas I'd bought at Macy's. As I walked into the living room, Scott reached out and pulled me into a tight embrace. He said he needed a hug and he was sure I needed one, too. Then we walked over to the table and ate the delicious dinner he brought with him.

For the rest of the night we watch movies on Netflix, joking around about life, eating junk food and getting to know each other. That night was the best time I had ever experienced. The night passed quickly. We fell asleep right on the sofa and didn't even realize it.

Waking up the next morning, I found Scott's strong, muscular arms wrapped around my waist, embracing his protection over me. Jumping up in shock, hoping nothing happened during the night, I pushed his arms off me... and he fell straight to the floor.

"What in the world happened last night?" I shouted, looking concerned.

"Whoa, you just going to knock a brother out?" He pulled himself up from the floor. "Nothing happened, Kendall. I would never take advantage of you like that," Scott replied. "I'm sorry. I lost track of time, I was supposed to leave last night."

"It's okay. I kind of enjoyed the laughter and dinner last night." I smiled up at him. At that moment, an intense feeling came over my body.

"Well, great, there's plenty more where that came from," he said, staring deeply into my eyes. I could feel the heat turning up intimately and felt something was about to happen. I quickly walked toward the bedroom with a sense of urgency to separate the distance between us. As soon as I closed the door and sat on the bed, I could hear the sound of the door swinging open as Scott rushed in.

Chapter EIGHT

"Kendall, I have to go. My mother was just rushed to the hospital, my father just called me."

Looking at Scott's face staring at me with a worried, painful look, I felt the need to help him in way.

"Whoa, what happened?"

"I'm not sure, but I have to go. Are you going to be all right here by yourself?" he asked.

"No," I frantically glanced around the room before continuing, "give me a second. I'm going with you."

"No, you don't have to, this is a family emergency. You have enough problems of your own."

I sighed and gave him a reassuring look that said I'm not taking no for an answer. "I'm going."

"Okay, okay ... Well, let's go." Scott gave me a strange look. "Are you sure, Kendall? Because you don't owe me anything, if that's what you think."

Clinching my jaw, I felt like he was trying to reject my help. So, I ran into the bathroom and quickly brushed my teeth. Once I put on a pair of joggers and a sweater, I brushed my hair down once more. "Let's go!" I said as I rushed toward the door, grabbing Scott's shirt.

"Dang," Scott said, holding his arms up in defeat. He was speechless with a wide-eyed look. We both jumped in the car to rush to the hospital.

The hospital was downtown New Orleans on Tulane Avenue, which was a good forty-five-minute drive with heavy eight o'clock rush hour traffic. As we got father down the highway, Scott started having an open conversation with me that I didn't expected. He told me more about his personal life.

"About one year ago I lost my fiancée. She was also my best friend, lover and motivator." He paused as if to calm himself. "On her way to our rehearsal dinner, she was involved in a two-collision car wreck that killed her instantly. After the tragedy, I found myself angry with God, until my mother encouraged me that God doesn't make mistakes and He is in control of all things. My mother quoted me a scripture from the Bible, 1Peter 5: 6-7, 'Humble yourselves, therefore, under God's mighty hand, that he may lift you up in due time. Cast all your anxiety on him because he cares for you.' That scripture really carried me over with the help of my mother and father being my spiritual leaders. My father couldn't give me as much as my mother because he was always busy pastoring his church. Sitting here, I'm thinking, what is God's plan in my life because I can't lose my mother," he said in a voice cracking with emotions. He laid his hand over my left thigh and then spoke with a soft tone. "Thank you."

My heartbeat quickened, pounding rapidly. I tried to ignore the tingling nerve endings where he touched me. Finally, we arrived at the hospital after wasting time trying to find a parking spot near the hospital. Scott shut the engine off and quickly got out of the car. We sprinted across the street to the entrance of the hospital. I looked at Scott and saw worry etched all over his face. Within five minutes we were on the elevator, heading up to the 2nd floor where they had his mother stationed. Once we made to the 2nd floor, we made a slight left and his mother's room was on the corner of the hall. We entered his mother's room with urgency, only to find that she wasn't in there. As we looked around the room, in a corner by the window, there was Scott's father, Pastor Howard Kodak. He was kneeled down on the floor praying by her bed. We quickly turned around and walked out the room, so we wouldn't interrupt his prayer with God. We started to exit the room to see if we could get updated information on his mother from one of the staff or nurses in the hospital.

"You are leaving already?" Scott's father asked. Scott's father was sixty-two years old, slim, 6'3, with bronze-colored skin tone. He had the brightest coffee-brown colored eyes, with platinum shaggy hair, and he was clean shaved with a well-groomed goatee. Stopping immediately, Scott nodded his head and turned around to face his father. His father hadn't even stood up yet, but it didn't surprise Scott that his father didn't have to see him to feel his presence. His father has always had a strong spiritual discernment and knew when things were going on around him without even looking.

Scott sighed. "Hey, dad, I didn't want to interrupt you."

"I was just talking to the father."

"Where is mother? Is she still in surgery?" Scott asked his father as he walked over to him. Slowly, his father pushed himself to his feet and met him halfway, while spreading his arms wide to give him a hug. Scott walked up to him and they wrapped their arms around each other in a loving embrace. His father exhaled, took a deep breath, and slowly lifted his eyes to look Scott directly in his eyes.

"Son, your mother is gone to be with the Lord," his voice cracked. "She didn't make it through the surgery. Her heart wasn't strong enough to endure it."

When I heard those words, I immediately slapped my hand over my mouth in shock because I wasn't expecting that, and I know Scott wasn't either. Scott was in shock. He leaned against the wall trembling, while shaking his head. Watching the tears flowing down Scott and his father's face, Scott fell to the floor.

"No, No! Why my momma?" Scott said, moaning, while slapping his knees in pain. I sniffed and quickly realized that I was in tears with them, like I personally knew her. I wiped the tears from my eyes and handed Mr. Kodak a couple of Kleenex from a box that was sitting on the night table near the bed. His father extended his hand to take the Kleenex and winked his eye at me, releasing an appreciative sigh. I couldn't bear to stay in the room any longer. I quickly walked toward the door, questioning my presence and why God allowed me to be here with this man during this time. As I walked out the door to head toward the elevator, I heard a familiar voice that sounded a lot like Larry. With no hesitation, I took a risk and followed the sound of the voice to see if it was really him. I tilted my head in the doorway; I was inconspicuous enough where I was sure I wouldn't be seen. Sure enough, it was Larry in the hospital room with his arms wrapped over the shoulder of a beautiful young Hispanic girl. She looked like she'd just stepped off the cover of a magazine.

Besides that, she also looked to be about five months pregnant!

Chapter NINE

Desiring to move closer and grab Larry and knock him upside his head, I felt myself trying to gasp for breath. I was totally in shock at what I was seeing.

The woman pressed her fingers against his lips to silence him.

"Calm down, honey," the women said to Larry as she rubbed her hands over her stomach.

"Listen, Doc, will my baby be okay?" Larry asked the doctor in a concerned tone. When I heard those words 'MY BABY' coming from my husband's voice, my heart started pounding, then my vision became blurred. I had to mentally order myself to calm down and relax.

I turned away from the room. In my haste to get away from the scene I had just witnessed between my husband and his obvious mistress, or baby's mother-to-be, I felt weak in the knees. I stumbled into a nurses' cart outside of the patient's door, knocking it, medication and several other items onto the floor. I felt overwhelmed, like the hospital walls were closing in on me. Walking in jerky, self-contained strides, a nurse came and helped me right before I almost collapsed. Everything appeared to be moving in slow motion. I could see the nurse's mouth moving, but I couldn't hear the words coming out. I started shaking my head, not having the ability to formulate words. Then... everything went dark as my body fell to the floor.

I must have been out for about fifteen minutes when I opened my eyes to see Larry walking out of the hospital room holding his mistress's hand. He hadn't noticed it was me that the nurses were helping, but somehow, I found the strength to jump to my feet. I ran over and grabbed my husband by the back of his shirt where he and his mistress stood waiting for the elevator. I had caught Larry by surprise, and he tried to pull away from me.

"Larry! What is going on here?!" My breathing was out of control, my nostrils flared, and I was sweating. I know I must have looked like a crazy person as I stood my ground in front of them.

"Whoa, Kendall?" I could tell by the sound of Larry's voice he never expected to see me standing there. "Why are you here?"

"You are lying piece of shi..." I launched myself at Larry, ready to attack his face, but two hands suddenly wrapped themselves around my waist, stopping me from attacking him. I struggled to break free.

"It's okay, keep calm," Scott's voice whispered in my ear as he picked me up and placed me on the other side of him, to put some distance between Larry and I. Taking short fast breaths, I tried to calm down. My body felt overheated, but I stood there giving Larry a wide-eyed look as I waited for him to explain himself before I did something bad to him.

"It's not what you think, Kendall." Larry said, clearing his throat and avoiding eye contact with me.

"Cut the crap, Larry!" I screamed. "It is what I see, you here with your pregnant mistress!" I began to struggle again, trying to break free of the strong arms holding me still, so that I could punch Larry in his smug face.

The elevator doors opened, and Larry walked inside, following behind his mistress, turning away from me. "Well, why you are asking, since you have it all figured out," Larry said, tugging on his tie.

I had never been so furious in my life. Trying to digest what he had just said pushed me over the edge. My face was flaming red and I could feel strands of hair sticking to the sweat and tears on my face. Managing to evade my captor for a moment, I reached down and grabbed my shoe to throw at him, but the elevator doors had shut before it got to him.

Turning away I burst out in a loud uncontrollable sob. Before I could get a chance to get any louder, Scott reached out and pulled me into his arms, wrapping his comforting arms around me, pressing his body against mine. He held me tightly, embracing my emotions.

"I'm here for you. It's okay. You deserve better," Scott said in a soothing tone. Releasing an appreciative sigh, I couldn't help but look deep into his eyes as he looked at me with sympathy. Feeling determined, my hands tightened on his cheeks as his eyes lowered back to my lips that parted in anticipation of his kiss.

"Scott?" Carol's voice came out of nowhere. I turned toward her, stepping away from Scott.

"Kendall, what's going on?" she said with a smirk on her face. I instantly groaned, knowing she was about to see Scott and I kiss.

"Is everything okay? How is your mother, Mr. Kodak? And, Kendall, why did I just see the bastard you call a husband down in the lobby holding a pregnant Latino's hands?" Carol said as her hands moved in jerks.

I looked back at Scott, startled, not knowing what to say, so I pulled Carol away to tell her everything that went on loud enough for her to hear. Scott had walked off after he had given me a go-ahead nod.

I sighed loudly and shook my head in shock

as I told Carol everything that had happened.

"Can you take me by my house and get my belongings, please?" I asked Carol as she rubbed my arms with her hand, doing her best to comfort me.

"Sure, do I need to stop and get my pistol? she said in an aggressive voice, smiling, trying to cheer me up.

Carol gave me the keys to her car so that I could wait downstairs while she went to pay her respects to her bosses.

Chapter TEN

After ten minutes Carol came and hopped in the car and we pulled out of the hospital parking lot. On the way back to my house, I couldn't stop thinking about what had happened and what had almost happened between Scott and me. How our lips were only millimeters apart from locking. I started believing that the feelings were mutual between us, with a sense that destiny was kicking in. Every thought that crossed my mind was all about Scott. I fantasized about him, craving more of the close affection we had shared.

When we finally arrived at my house, I got out the car and headed to the front door. When I went to put my key in the door, my key wouldn't fit, so I started punching my security code into the keypad to gain access to my house, but it failed as well. I started getting angry all over again when I realized that Larry had changed all of the locks, as well as the key codes, preventing me from entering my home. I immediately begin to yell Linda's name while beating on the door.

Linda opened the door.

"What? What's going on, Kendall? she asked with fear in her eyes. As I walked inside my house, I found all my stuff packed in boxes in the front entrance of my foyer. Larry had already had my belonging packed up. As soon as I saw my stuff packed, my blood started rushing to my head. At that moment, my entire Bible studies − anger, vengeance, hatred, etc. had been erased from my mind, because the thoughts I had for Larry were not godly at all. I looked at Linda and pushed her out of my way.

"I should be asking you what's going on? Did he have you do this?" I asked Linda, staring her dead in her eyes without blinking.

"Yes, he ordered me to do it immediately. But, Kendall, I didn't want anything to do with this. I'm sorry," Linda exclaimed. Carol walked into the house and saw my belongings in the middle of the front entrance.

"What is this? Kendall, tell me why your stuff is packed in front of this door like this. It is what I'm thinking it is," Carol said in an aggressive and angry voice. I squeezed my eyes shut after Carol stopped talking, hoping it was all just a bad dream. As I opened them, it was still there, then reality kicked in.

"Okay, enough is enough ... they say three strikes you're out! And Larry has struck out!" I could feel the anger and an evilness building inside of me. I had been faithful, honest and sincere to this man for two whole years, and now he felt it was okay to just kick me to the curve? Well, I guess I'm going to have to go back and do a re-run on How to Get Away with Murder to find a way to get rid of him and that mistress without getting caught, because this one I just can't let it ride.

Carol pulled me out of my thoughts as she moved closer to me to whisper in my ear. "Let's do a Rip Effect and turn this mother out!" Carol said, digging in her purse looking for something to use. I looked at Carol and started to have flashbacks on the last time we did a Rip Effect. It was done when we destroyed her ex-husband's Mercedes Benz. We ripped off everything we could until we got tired.

"Don't tempt me, Carol."

"You either forget this happened or take control of this situation and fight back," Carol said.

Without hesitation, I responded back quickly, "Let's do this!"

After sending Linda home and spending a full hour destroying my use-to-be home, we grabbed my things and left. Looking back, remembering some of the good times Larry and I had shared in that house, I realized that all the bad outweighed the good. I started to think, was it even meant to be?

"Are you okay, Kendall?" Carol asked. At once I just nodded yes, even though my heart felt like it had been ripped out and destroyed. Carol dropped me off at Scott's cabin, so Larry still couldn't trace me. Feeling rejected and abandoned, I went in, took a shower and crashed on the couch. Hours passed and I hadn't received a text or call from Scott, so I went to the computer to check and see if he'd sent an email. A weird feeling came over me. I started wondering why he hadn't called, texted or emailed me.

Unexpectedly, I went into the bedroom next to the guest room I was sleeping in and searched to find a picture of Scott. After looking for ten minutes, I came across a picture of Scott and his ex-fiancée. Looking at that picture of her was like I was looking through a mirror. She was identical to me. I couldn't help but think, was this fate or destiny? I grabbed the picture and took it and put it in the bedroom near my clothes, then I got a bottle of wine to calm my nerves, as I watched NCIS until I fell asleep on the couch.

Chapter ELEVEN

Five hours had passed and I glimpsed at my phone to see if Scott had called or text. Looking at my caller ID, I noticed there was a missed called from him. "Darnit!" I jumped up to try and call Scott back, but I heard keys rattling in the door. Scott walked in the door.

"Hey there, are you feeling better?" he asked, with a heavy sigh.

I answered, "Yes, now that you're here."

"Well, great, I just stopped by to check on you, Carol told me what Larry did. I just thought I'd let you know you can stay here as long as you want."

"Seriously, you came all the way over here just to tell me that? You could have told me that over the phone." Scott chuckled, looking at me intensely. He walked closer to me, then put his hands around my neck to pull me even closer. Gently, he placed a soft warm kiss on my neck. Suddenly, I felt like my body was literally on fire, blood boiling as he sensually placed more kisses. Before I knew it, his lips locked with mines in a passionate kiss. In my mind, I knew it was the wrong thing to do. I wanted to pull away, but I couldn't get his lips out of my thoughts. After a few blissful moments, with our lips still exploring each other's, he is grinding himself against me. Tearing off my clothes, his left hand traveled down in between my legs. He slid into me with pure sensation, touching every nerve in my body. With our bodies still joined, we slowly made our way to the bedroom breathing hard with my legs wrapped around him. For the next thirty minutes, we were in a zone; feeling strong sensations flowing through our bodies like never. Afterward, our bodies sweaty and hot, we laid back and exhaled deeply, exhausted, while the breeze from the ceiling fan cooled us off. Then we cuddled on the bed with the sheets between us, listening to each other's heartbeats. Suddenly, this strange looked flashed across Scott's face. He looked unnerved.

"What is it, you look spooked?"

"Wow," Scott said, scratching his head.

"Did I do something wrong?"

"No ... No." He grabbed me and held me close to him. "It's my mother and fiancée. I saw their faces."

"REALLY?"

"Yeah, I saw them clear as day."

"Well maybe it's a sign, they're watching over you."

"Maybe." He sat up and chuckled.

"I'm going to go take a shower, bae," I said as I got out of the bed, wrapping the sheets around my body to cover up.

"Okay, do you want me to take one with you... let me clean you?"

I sighed with no hesitation "Sure, I'd like that; no more damage can be done. Matter of fact, can you take off tomorrow and keep me company?"

"Wow, it looks like someone is already getting spoiled. I already had the days off, so your wish has been granted," Scott replied with a humorless chuckle.

After that day my life totally changed. It had been several months since his mother's burial and my separation. Our undeniably hot lovemaking continued. Things were falling in place for me. I was able to get a divorce from Larry and was awarded half of our assets. I also kept the restraining order against him. I wasn't bothered with Larry anymore; he had moved on with his mistress in another state and sold our home.

During that time Scott and I spent countless time together going on adventures, shopping, traveling and so much more. The feelings I had for Scott had become stronger and stronger. I was constantly thinking of him every three seconds, I had to see him or be with him. Was I falling in love? Or was its obsession? I didn't know because there is a very thin line between them.

It was a normal Saturday morning and we were scheduled to meet up the gym to workout out. But that morning I couldn't keep anything down. I literally stayed in the bathroom all morning throwing up. For the next couple of hours, Scott never called to check on me to see why I hadn't arrived. That wasn't like him. It seemed that the last few days at the office – and even out of the office – we hadn't been as close as we were usually. He always had lame excuses, like Larry, saying he was too busy. Finally, after three hours of feeling nausea and sick, I felt well enough to get up and drive.

I got in my car and started driving. I picked up my phone to call him, but the call went to his voice mail as usual. When I arrived at the gym, Scott was nowhere to be found, but his car was still in the parking lot. So I decided to wait in the car until he showed up. After twenty minutes of waiting, my nausea returned, so I hurried into the gym to use the restroom. Once my stomach was settled, I walked out the gym to see Scott getting out of a pearl white 2016 model Infinity with dark tinted windows.

Chapter TWELVE

I quickly walked up to him before he got into his car.

"Scott!" I yelled in a blunt voice.

"Kendall, I was just about to call you and see what happened to you this morning."

"Yeah, I bet." I smirked.

"I'm guessing you are upset," Scott said as he sighs.

"I've been sick all morning, literally feeling like I was dying, and you didn't even bother to check and see where I was at. Well, yes, Scott, your guess is correct. I am highly upset."

"I'm sorry, Kendall. Let me take you to lunch. I have something very important that I must tell you."

Scott took my hand and we walked over to a restaurant next door to the gym. As we waited to be seated, I realized that Scott was avoiding eye contact with me, so I started sensing something was wrong and I felt light-headed. Once we were seated, and the waitress took our orders, Scott began telling me he had something to tell me. Of course, I knew it was something bad, but I listened. He took my hand and held it, gazing into my eye.

"I've been discussing with my father about how my mother keeps appeared to me in a vision, and we think it's best for us to move on with our life. My father and I discovered that ever since we've been together, both of our relationship with God is not the same. I've been a stumbling block in your way with God and I can't take the guilt any longer," he said sadly.

I couldn't hold back my tears any longer. Feeling overheated, I started fanning myself.

"This can't be happening, not now, Scott. We've only been together for a couple of months.

There's so much I want to do with you!" I said sobbing.

He grabbed me and we hugged one another. I couldn't stand to continue to look at him without getting angry and emotional, so I got up and left the restaurant.

A small voice started speaking in my head as I was driving home. It was telling me that Scott and I were meant to be, and I can't let him go. Immediately, I didn't shake that voice off me, I just reacted and turned around to head back to the restaurant where Scott was. When I arrived, Scott was just pulling off, so I slowed my car down so I could trail him without him knowing it. After fifteen minutes of trailing him throughout the city, he finally pulled in at his father's house. I hesitated to get out of my car, so I kept going and drove to his house and parked on the side corner where it was visible enough for me to see him, but not him see me.

After waiting a good hour, he finally showed up at his house. So, I pulled off to head to the office so I could get a copy of his schedules for the next couple of weeks. I know it was crazy, but I refused to be used again; that was in my mind, so I did everything in my power to make it happen. I got his schedule from the office that night and went home to cuddle up with one of his pictures I had. I was getting sicker and sicker, mentally and physically and didn't know what was going on with me.

Monday morning came I didn't show up for work. I went to the doctor to find out I was pregnant. What a surprise to me. After two years, I never would have imagined I would be pregnant since the doctor told me I couldn't bear any kids my last pregnancy. I was so excited, but hurt at the same time, because I knew Scott was the father.

I decided not to tell him, because I didn't want him to think I planned this just to trap him. My plans were to stay in touch with him secretly, so I did. Eventually, I quit my job because I got tired of being ignored by him, but I still planted myself in his path for months. I hung around the gym when he went. I cased the bar where he hung out every Friday night. I drove past his house at least three times a day. I set up several Facebook and Twitter account to keep up with him. This behavior had gotten so unhealthy that I knew I needed to get some help. I didn't realize the line was so thin between love and obsession. I realized that my whole life revolved around Scott and I was commitment to a non-existing relationship that had to be stopped.

Chapter THIRTEEN

Finally, I had made up my mind to stop my obsessive behavior. But what I didn't realize is that without God, I couldn't break any unhealthy patterns. It took the last episode for me to finally see it. I went about my daily duty of following Scott, but this time, I ran up on something I couldn't handle.

Carol and Scott were in a relationship that I didn't know about. As hard as I tried to back-track or try to figure out what I had missed, I couldn't figure it out. The only conclusion was that they must have kept it inside the office only. They arrived at the park, and once there,

I watched as he proposed to Carol. I couldn't breathe, my heart was pounding rapidly. I fought within myself mentally trying to maintain control. A spirit of rage came across my body, I pressed on the gas pedal and drove off in anger. Momentarily forgetting I'm pregnant, my blood rushed through my body with anger, which caused me to immediately slam on my brakes and burst out with a scream like never. I was at the point I was angry with everyone, including God – questioning my reasons for still living on this earth.

Later that night I went into a mad woman's rage. I wanted to do a Rip Effect on Scott and Carol. I had feelings of being rejected, yet again, by others that I thought loved me, and this made me very upset. I set my alarm clock to wake me up at three o'clock in the morning. Once I lie down, it felt like I had only gotten an hour of sleep because it went by so fast. I jumped out of the bed, showered, put on my clothes and got in my car. I planned to arrive at Scott's house and tell him about my pregnancy. Once I made it to his house, I entered his front door with the key I had copied a couple of month ago. I walked toward his bedroom door and I heard the shower running. Slowly, walking in the bedroom I sat on his bed, waiting for him to come out. Startled, Scott jumped slightly when he saw me sitting on his bed.

"What in the world are you doing, Kendall? How did you get in my house?" he said, walking to the door to reach for his phone. He didn't know I had already taken it. I took a step forward, toward him.

"Why?" my voice cracked in pain. "Why did you go behind my back and have a relationship with my best friend? After everything I have already been through, why would you do that to me?" I was now sobbing, and barely able to see through my tears. As I got closer, I pulled out my gun and forced him to get dressed, then I tied him up and made him get in my car. I drove to his family's cottage where everything had started. Once we arrived, I made him get out the car and I grabbed a bag I had on the back seat, which contained ropes, tape, a flashlight and my ultrasound. We entered the house and I ordered him to sit down on the chair, while I tried to tie him up.

"Kendall, what are you doing? How is this going to solve anything?" Scott asked as he followed my orders.

"I'm not trying to solve anything; I just want to get my point across. I'm sick and tired of being rejected by others and feeling abandoned," I exclaimed, becoming very still looking at him.

"Kendall, what point? I told you this not what God planned for us, I was a hindering you. I did it because I love you and I still do. But it's loves from a distance."

With spontaneous laughter I looked at him repeating the same thing over and over.

"Love doesn't abandon you. Love is willing to have your life complicated by the needs and struggles of the others. Love is a promise, love is a souvenir, once given it is never forgotten and you cannot let it disappear. Love is an untamed force. We try to control it, it destroys us. When we try to imprison it, it enslaves us. When we try to understand it, it leaves us feeling lost, broken and confused. That's what you've done to me, Scott. Love is sacrificing to keep your family together no matter what."

"Family, what family? We have no family together," Scott replied with a confused looked.

"I'm sorry you think we don't, but we do. You see, we are having a daughter, and I refuse to let her be abandoned and alone in this world like me. You will love her and take care of her, that's why I have you here, because I love you so much, I'm risking everything," I said as tears began to flow down my face. The more the tears flowed, the angrier I got.

"Okay, Kendall, I am so thankful we're having a child together, but having her in prison won't solve anything. It will only cause hurt to all of us. Kendall, love does not hurt, and jealously is not love. Jealously is fear. Love never drives people to kill or worry. That's OBSESSION, Kendall. You must be able to differentiate between them. You can be confused because the line is just that thin, but please untie me and let's make this work and stop with this psycho stuff. Love is greater than both of us. God is love, and you know this, Kendall. This is not the Kendall I met, she was a God-fearing woman who guarded herself with the Word of God. Now you have allowed the enemy to overtake your body. God made me leave you, I was fighting it because my purpose wasn't to fall in love with you, it was to push you to your calling," Scott said, his voice cracked as tears start flowing down his face.

So many thoughts came across my mind. My eyes were damp with emotions. Feeling confused, I stared at Scott, then looked at the gun in my hand, then I heard a click.

Chapter FOURTEEN

As I clicked the gun's safety, I felt my pulse pounding. Conflicting emotions of the passion I have for Scott clashed with my anger at myself for what I was doing. Even while my body lost itself in the lustful pleasure. I hated that I had easily allowed my emotions to make me quickly forget my belief and go into backsliding. I had internal burning pain of me to quickly let sex dictate my life. I hated the ground I walked on for what I had done and was doing. I kept trying to remind myself repeatedly: The wages of sin are death;

the wages of sin are death. I knew that eventually I would die anyway. So, I raised the gun, pointed it toward my head and tightly closed my eyes. Not knowing during all my thoughts and attempting to commit suicide, Scott was breaking a free of his restraints.

"No, Kendall!" Scott exploded in a heart pounding release of scriptures.

"For I know the thoughts that I think toward you, saith the Lord, thoughts of peace and not of evil, to give you an expected end. - Jeremiah 29:11."

"Eyes have not seen, nor ears heard, nor have entered into the heart of man the things which God has prepared for us. - 1Corinthians 2:9"

"For I will be merciful to their unrighteousness, and their sins and their iniquities will I remember no more. Hebrew8:12."

As he was reciting the scriptures, a radiant glow appeared to me, speaking in a soft voice, telling me to spread the gospel of Jesus and be a living testimony to others. I could still hear Scott quoting the scripture with passion. I opened my eyes, and with no warning, Scott leaped over toward me and grabbed the gun. I looked into his eyes that were so bright and glossy.

He grabbed me and held me so tight and started crying. I could feel the genuine love he had for me through that moment. We held each other for about five minutes, praying for one another.

After the prayer, and me being a back to the right state of mind, Scott explained that his mother prayed that same prayers over him when he was at that same low point in his life of wanting to give up. He continued to speak.

"One month before we ran into each other at the gym, I had already been following you. One day, about a month after my fiancée's death, my mother and I saw you at the grocery store. I couldn't take my eyes off you. My mother explained to me that you were in danger and it was my destiny to push you to your future. As the days went by, I was hesitant to approach you until that day. I didn't know we were going to fall in love with one another. That's why my mother appeared to me in the vision after we made love, because she knew I had got out of God's will. Kendall, that's why I ended our relationship, we were supposed to be just friends. That's all, but I allowed my flesh to take over. I just wanted to be close to someone again and you looked like my fiancée; I couldn't resist you. Please forgive me for not telling you this. I stopped running from my calling and I surrendered to God. Now I want you to do the same. I would like for us to start over and leave it as friendship and raise our daughter together." Scott sighed deeply as he finished speaking.

I was in so much shock I couldn't move an inch. I was in disbelief. I couldn't believe what I had just heard. Pressing my hand against my chest, I surrendered that day.

Six months later, I had our six-pound, eight-ounce baby girl. We named her Destiny Kodak. Throughout the whole six months, Scott never missed a doctor's appointment. He was so supportive every step of the way.

One year later, Scott and Carol got married. He was now pastoring his father's church. My best friend, Carol got saved and was now a wonderful first lady. As for me, little Destiny and I are traveling the world, preaching the gospel, doing women seminars. God allowed me to start a strong international women's group that has been anointed and productive called "DESTINY'S WILL" (Women Inspiring Life's Legacy). Linda is now my personal housekeeper and she lives with Destiny and me. Now I am strongly in love with my life; it couldn't have been any better. So just think about it. It all started with a little love that crossed over to a thin line of obsession that pushed me to progression to figure out what my destiny was. Now, I'm fully working for God and waiting patiently until he sends me the king that he created to be my husband. The one that will love me and treat me as a queen.

Erica T Sherrill

OR

"Erica T Capri

Erica T Sherrill is the author behind A Thin Line Trilogy Series. She is a stylist, film producer, entrepreneur, and playwright. Her work as playwright has become popular over the years with her production performing at Colleges and theatre stages. She's the rock star mother of two young children and CEO of Gemlight Publishing LLC. Erica wrote over twenty pieces in the combination of stage plays, screenplays, children fiction, and novels. She has no plans to stop writing and hard at work on her book and film releases.

Follow the Author:

Facebook: Author Erica T Sherrill

Linkedin: Erica T Sherrill

Email: ericasherrill77@gmail.com

Other Titles by the Author

To Purchase more books visit:

www.gemlightpublishing.com

Upcoming Title;

"How to Invest To Be Bless"(Self-help)

"Five Senses to Love " (Women's Empowerment)

"Today Is The Day !"(Children's Fiction)

2nd Edition Entitled

" A Thin Line Between Love

& Fear"

On sale now !!

ISBN# 978-17344326-3-3

Interested in joining our Gemlight Publishing family? Visit our website for more details!

www.gemlightpublishing.com

Follow Us on Social Media ;
Facebook,Instagram,LinkedIn,& Twitter

Gemlight Publishing LLC Company

Attn: Erica T Sherrill /Publisher

gemlightpublishingllc@gmail.com

49 Hardy Court, Suite 385

Gulfport, MS 39507

228-233-5455 /Office

ERICA T CAPRI
A thin line between
LOVE &
FEAR
Unravel Series

A thin line between LOVE & FEAR

(Unravel Series)

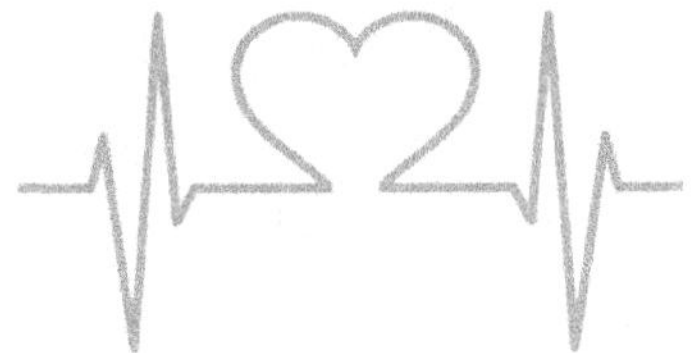

Erica T. Capri

A thin line between LOVE & FEAR

Refreshed and newly divorced, Kendall Alexander fortuitously encounters a handsome man during a flight for her business to New York City. Reeling from mixed emotions caused by her previous marriage, forced to revisit a past filled with scorn, shame, and infidelity. Upon arriving in New York, Kendall has an unexpected encounter with her ex-husband, Larry, revealing a shocking secret – a child unknowingly born of her frozen embryo!

Kendall redirects her efforts, seeking answers and sets a course to fight back and expose the vicious crimes committed against her. She continues to question the magnitude of the unfairness of her life and is determined not to be defeated a second time. Will Kendall escape her fears and fight? Or will she take the risk and face the terror of life?

In A Thin Line Between Love & Fear Unravel, provides an unflinching look at crime, love, and deceit.

Prologue

Years have passed by like a whirlwind. My daughter Destiny was born and now has grown up to be a gorgeous little princess. All the wounds from my broken marriage and the incident with Scott have faded away.

My life has become God's and Destiny's

world, doing things to please Him and cherishing moments with my daughter.

I've spent a lot a time throughout the years traveling, doing full time ministry and motivational speaking with my women's group, Destiny's Will. God has opened so many doors for me to travel and explore the world, and to help so many women in dealing with depression, domestic violence, abuse, and relationship struggles. Scott and I have developed close friendship for the sake of our daughter.

My baby girl Destiny is now two years old. Every day I'm breathing I am thanking God that I could see her **grow**, see her first steps, and hear her first words.

Destiny is my miracle. After multiple miscarriages, struggling with depression, and doctors telling me that it was impossible for me to carry a child, let alone deliver one without problems, I was blessed with the perfect baby girl. I am so honored and grateful to have Destiny, and to carry and deliver her without complications. She has the most beautiful curly hair, brown eyes, bronze skin, and the voice of an angel. To me, her hugs are worth more than millions of dollars. Every second I'm without my little princess, travelhair, brown eyes, bronze skin, and the voice of an angel. To me, her hugs are worth more than millions of dollars. Every second I'm without my little princess, traveling for work or something, breaks my heart until I can see her again. Now it's summertime, and I have a women's event in New York that will require me to stay for a week. During that time, I know I'll need strength while I'm away from my baby. but the little freedom will give me a little 'Me Time'.

Thank you for your support. I hope so far you have enjoyed the story. The 2nd Edition is now available to purchase, please get your copy and see what happened to Kendall and her new life!

Best wishes,

Erica